For Donna

To Marilyn with very best wishes
David Wisniewski MARCH 16, 1997

Clarion Books ◆ a Houghton Mifflin Company imprint ◆ 215 Park Avenue South, New York, NY 10003 ◆ Text and illustrations copyright © 1996 by David Wisniewski ◆ The illustrations for this book were executed in Color-Aid, Coral, and Bark cut papers ◆ The text is set in 16/20-point Dante medium. ◆ All rights reserved. ◆ For information about permission to reproduce selections from this book, write to Permissions, Houghton Mifflin Company, 215 Park Avenue South, New York, NY 10003. ◆ For information about this and other Houghton Mifflin trade and reference books and multimedia products, visit The Bookstore at Houghton Mifflin on the World Wide Web at (http://www.hmco.com/trade/). ◆ Printed in the U.S.A. ◆ Library of Congress Cataloging-in-Publication Data ◆ Wisniewski, David. Golem / written and illustrated by David Wisniewski. p. cm. Summary: A saintly rabbi miraculously brings to life a clay giant who helps him watch over the Jews of sixteenth-century Prague. ISBN 0-395-72618-2 1. Golem. 2. Judah Loew ben Bezalel, ca. 1525–1609—Legends. 3. Legends, Jewish. [1. Golem. 2. Jews—Czech Republic—Folklore. 3. Folklore—Czech Republic.] I. Title. BM531.W57 1996 398.21'089924—dc20 [E] 95-21777 CIP AC
BVG 10 9 8 7 6 5 4 3 2 1

Photography of cut-paper illustrations by Lee Salsbery

GOLEM

STORY AND PICTURES BY DAVID WISNIEWSKI

Clarion Books/New York

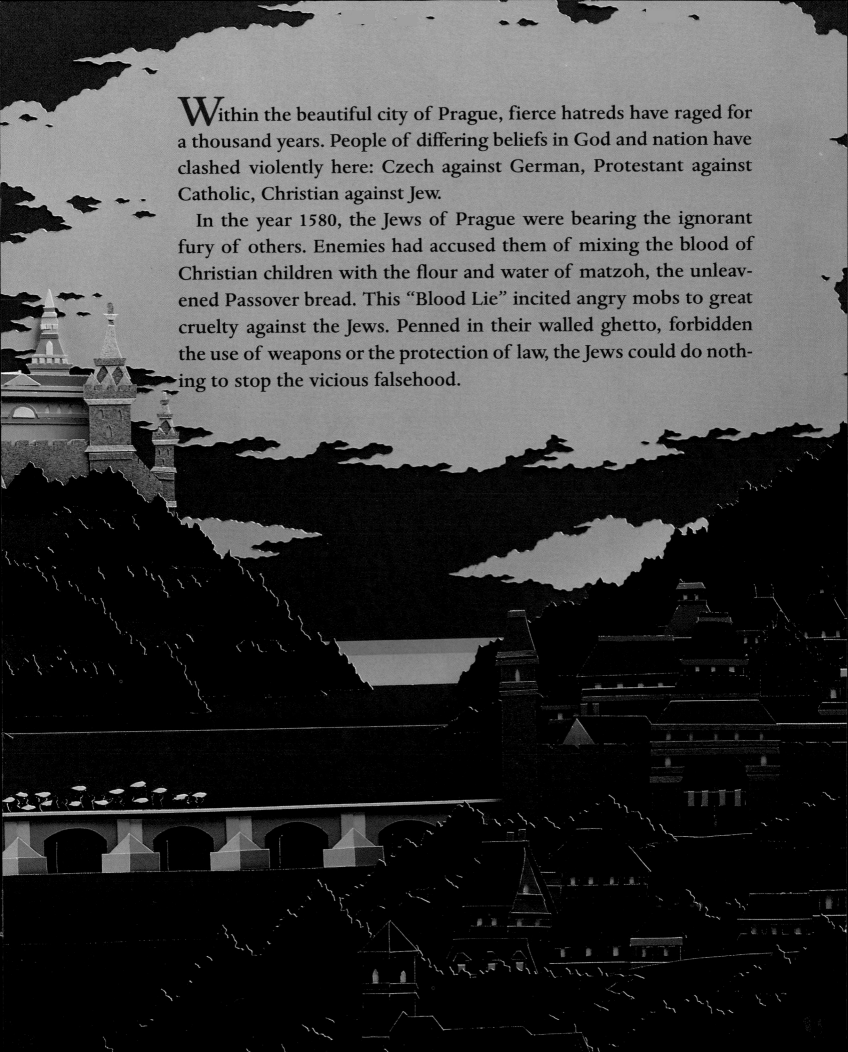

Within the beautiful city of Prague, fierce hatreds have raged for a thousand years. People of differing beliefs in God and nation have clashed violently here: Czech against German, Protestant against Catholic, Christian against Jew.

In the year 1580, the Jews of Prague were bearing the ignorant fury of others. Enemies had accused them of mixing the blood of Christian children with the flour and water of matzoh, the unleavened Passover bread. This "Blood Lie" incited angry mobs to great cruelty against the Jews. Penned in their walled ghetto, forbidden the use of weapons or the protection of law, the Jews could do nothing to stop the vicious falsehood.

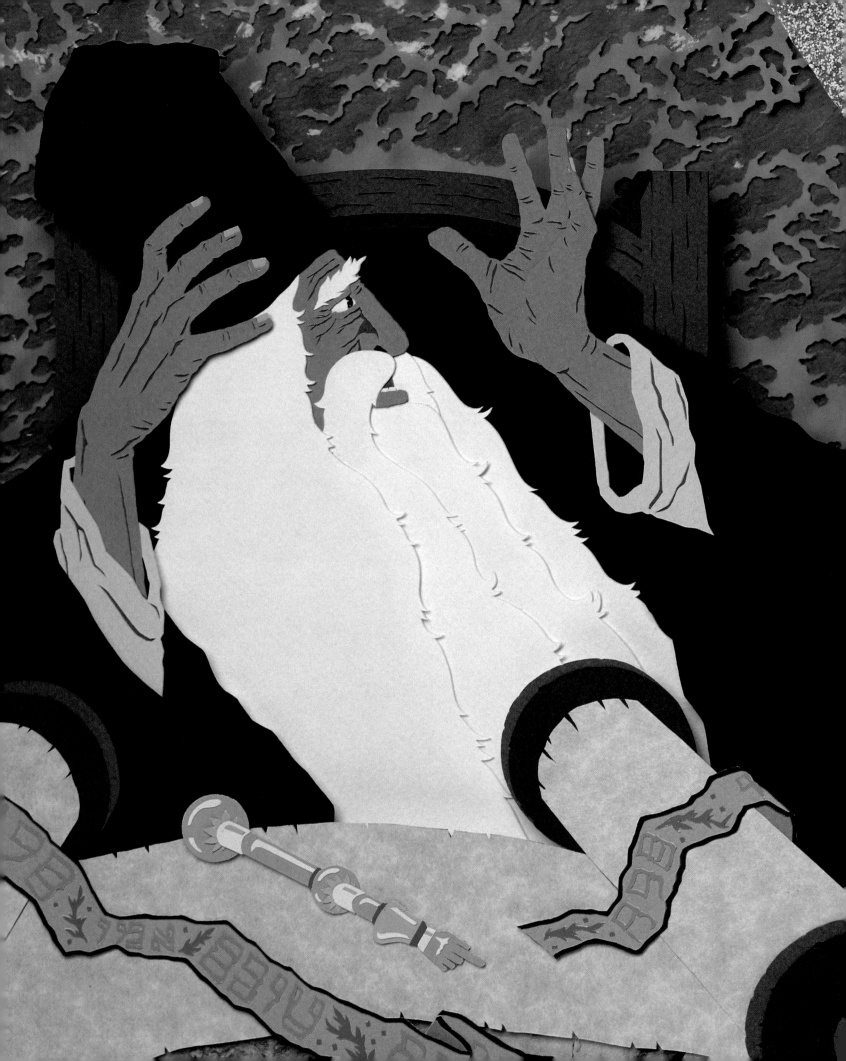

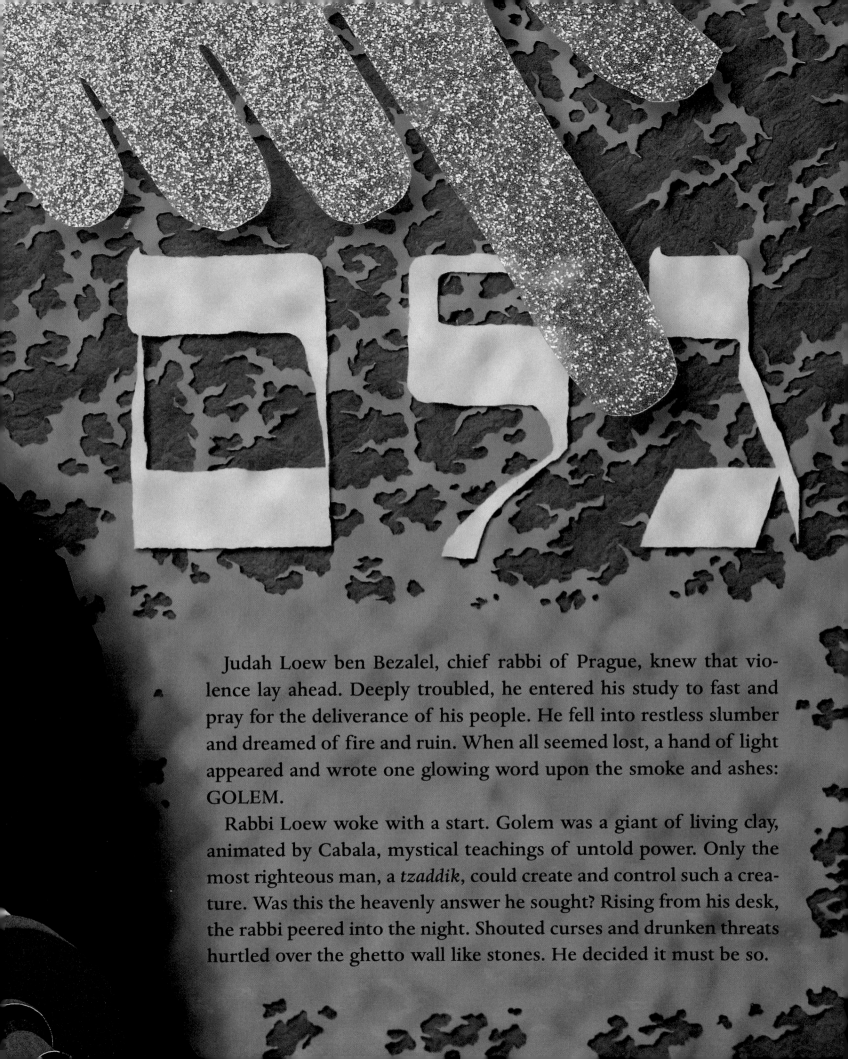

Judah Loew ben Bezalel, chief rabbi of Prague, knew that violence lay ahead. Deeply troubled, he entered his study to fast and pray for the deliverance of his people. He fell into restless slumber and dreamed of fire and ruin. When all seemed lost, a hand of light appeared and wrote one glowing word upon the smoke and ashes: GOLEM.

Rabbi Loew woke with a start. Golem was a giant of living clay, animated by Cabala, mystical teachings of untold power. Only the most righteous man, a *tzaddik*, could create and control such a creature. Was this the heavenly answer he sought? Rising from his desk, the rabbi peered into the night. Shouted curses and drunken threats hurtled over the ghetto wall like stones. He decided it must be so.

In the morning, Rabbi Loew sent for his son-in-law, Itzak Kohen, and his best student, Yakov Sassoon. He explained the dream and asked their help. "As the divine Name, the *ha-Shem*, created us through words, so we must create Golem," he said. "Now pray and purify yourselves, for this night we must use the Holy Name of God."

When darkness fell, the three men left the ghetto through a secret

opening in the wall. They hurried along the forbidden avenues of
Prague to the cold clay banks of the river Vltava. Itzak and Yakov
began to dig.

By midnight, an enormous mound of clay lay before the rabbi.
Praying softly, he plunged his hands into the vast lump, shaping it.
Hours later, he arose and stood back. A crude clay giant lay lifeless
on the riverbank.

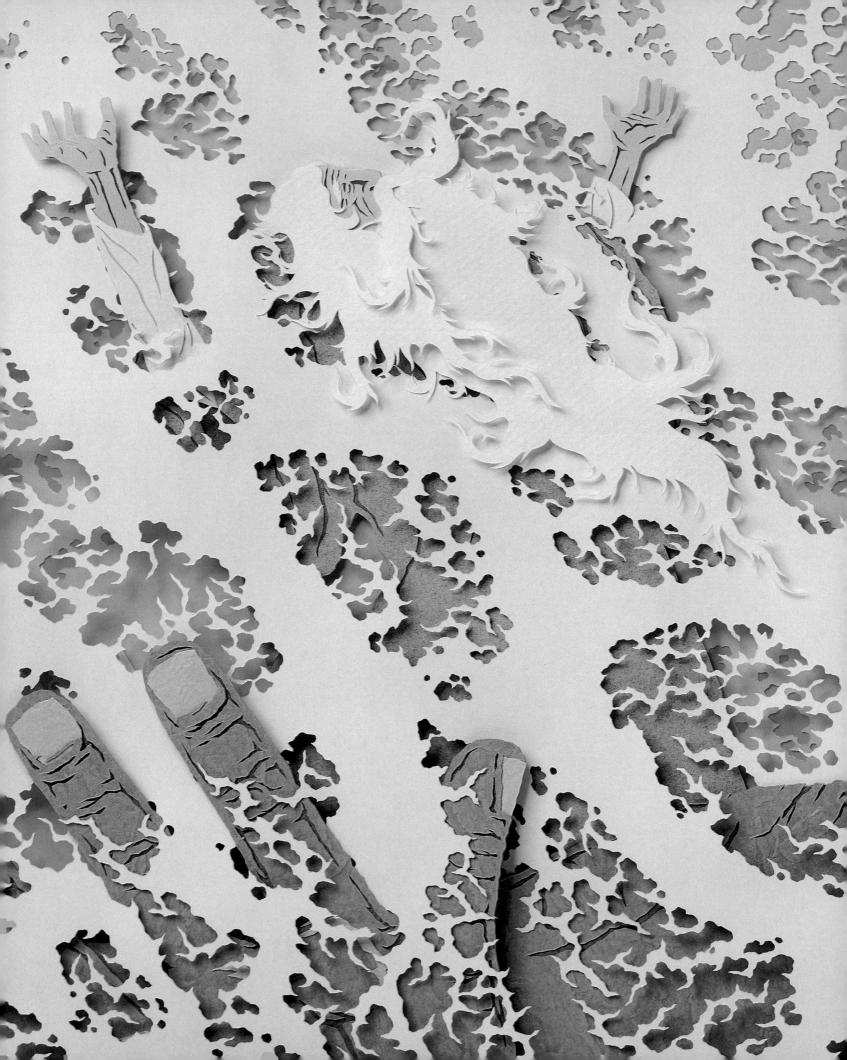

Raising his arms, Rabbi Loew chanted *zirufim*, mighty spells from Cabala. The words soared aloft and unleashed the power of Life itself. As lightning strikes iron and flashes to earth, so the infinite energy of creation blazed though the rabbi into the coarse clay.

Staggering, the rabbi lifted his arms higher and uttered the Holy Name. Howling wind and torrential rain lashed down. Writhing columns of steam shrieked from the figure. Itzak and Yakov gripped each other in terror.

When the tumult ceased, the three men advanced over the hissing ground. There, wreathed in vapor, lay a giant man, complete and perfect.

The rabbi knelt and engraved the word *emet*—Truth—upon the creature's forehead. Instantly, the giant's chest expanded like bellows. A deep breath shuddered from his lips.

"Golem!" commanded the rabbi. "Awake!"

Golem's eyes opened, murky and unblinking. "Father," his great voice rumbled, "was this wise to do?"

"We shall know soon enough," answered Rabbi Loew. "Now stand. Wrap this cloak about yourself and follow us." In the darkness before dawn, four returned to the ghetto.

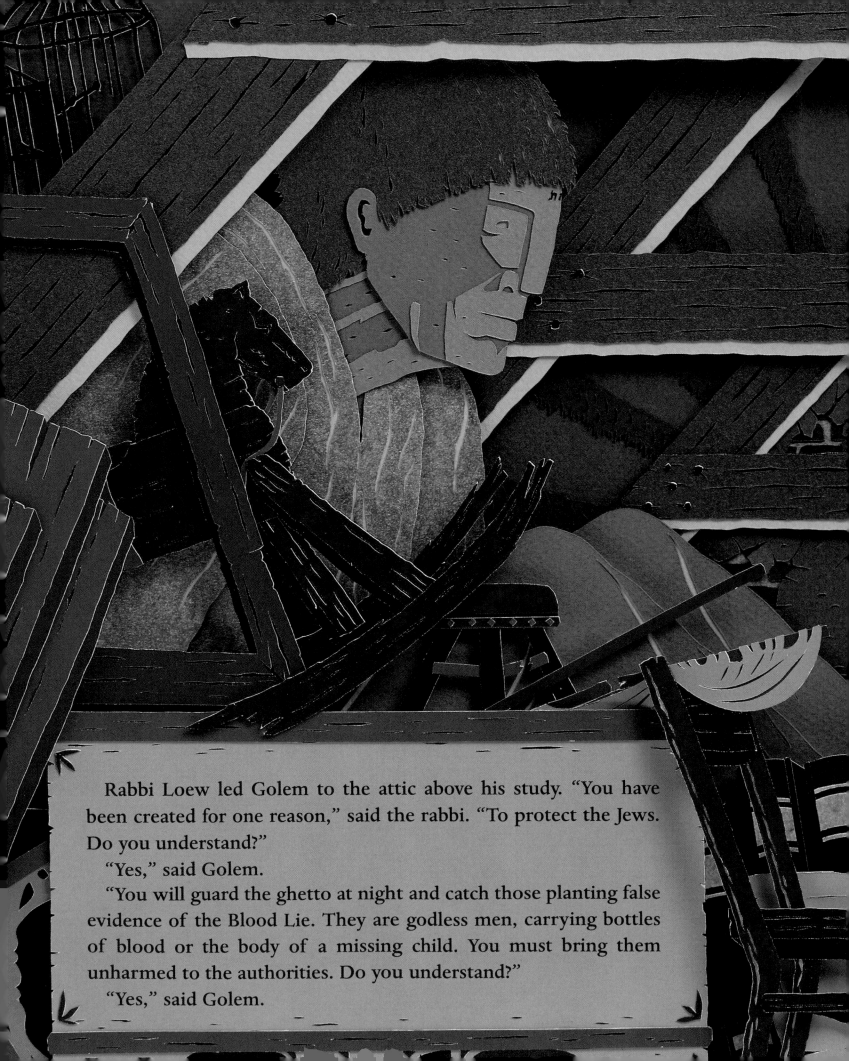

Rabbi Loew led Golem to the attic above his study. "You have been created for one reason," said the rabbi. "To protect the Jews. Do you understand?"

"Yes," said Golem.

"You will guard the ghetto at night and catch those planting false evidence of the Blood Lie. They are godless men, carrying bottles of blood or the body of a missing child. You must bring them unharmed to the authorities. Do you understand?"

"Yes," said Golem.

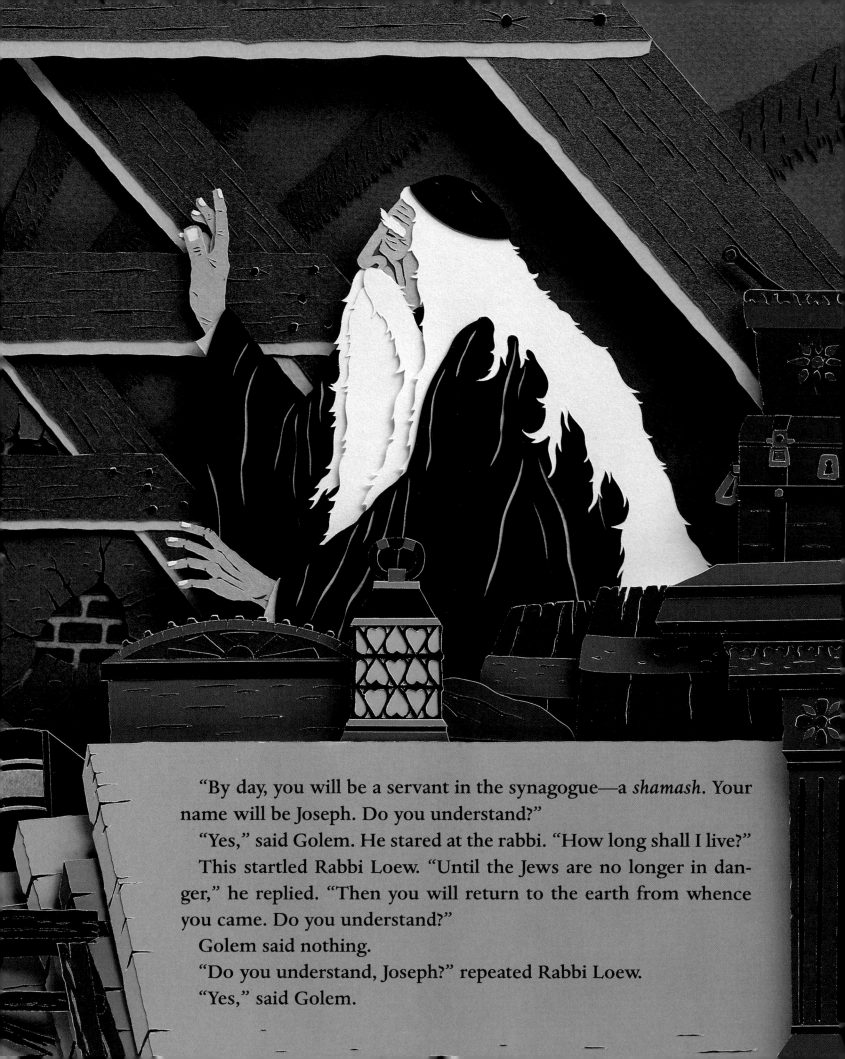

"By day, you will be a servant in the synagogue—a *shamash*. Your name will be Joseph. Do you understand?"

"Yes," said Golem. He stared at the rabbi. "How long shall I live?"

This startled Rabbi Loew. "Until the Jews are no longer in danger," he replied. "Then you will return to the earth from whence you came. Do you understand?"

Golem said nothing.

"Do you understand, Joseph?" repeated Rabbi Loew.

"Yes," said Golem.

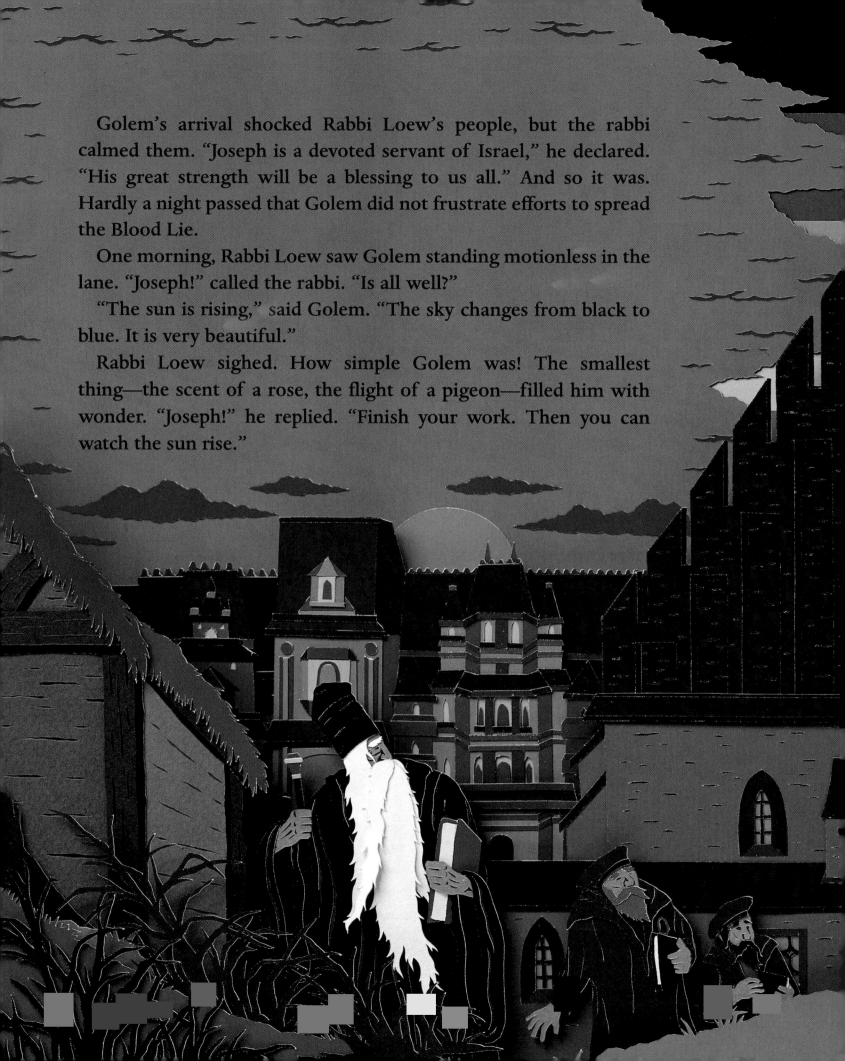

Golem's arrival shocked Rabbi Loew's people, but the rabbi calmed them. "Joseph is a devoted servant of Israel," he declared. "His great strength will be a blessing to us all." And so it was. Hardly a night passed that Golem did not frustrate efforts to spread the Blood Lie.

One morning, Rabbi Loew saw Golem standing motionless in the lane. "Joseph!" called the rabbi. "Is all well?"

"The sun is rising," said Golem. "The sky changes from black to blue. It is very beautiful."

Rabbi Loew sighed. How simple Golem was! The smallest thing—the scent of a rose, the flight of a pigeon—filled him with wonder. "Joseph!" he replied. "Finish your work. Then you can watch the sun rise."

With the jail full of Golem's arrests, the thoughtful people of Prague began to see the Blood Lie for the slander it was. This enraged the enemies of the Jews. They gathered a mob and marched to the ghetto, hoping to start a riot.

Rabbi Loew summoned Golem and hurried to the gates of the ghetto. The giant seemed taller than before; the rabbi could barely see the mark of Truth on his forehead.

With a hail of bricks and curses, the mob arrived and stormed the gates. The massive doors swayed but held. Golem stood before them. The Jews, outnumbered and weaponless, waited silently.

Then a jeering cry went up. A battering ram had arrived. At each blow, wood splintered. Hinges wailed in protest. Still Golem stood . . . but taller, much taller. Rabbi Loew could see him grow.

Then the gates came crashing down. The mob poured into the ghetto.

The first wave of attackers screamed in terror when they saw Golem looming above them. With the back of his hand, he swept them aside. Still the rabble surged in, propelled by those in back. Golem took hold of the battering ram and, snapping it in two, raked great furrows in the crowd.

Rabbi Loew covered his eyes. This was too much destruction, too much.

Leaving the dead and wounded, the mob fled in panic. Golem threw the broken battering ram after them. He lifted the shattered gates and hung them back on their ruined hinges. Then he plodded back into the ghetto.

The next day, Rabbi Loew was summoned to Prague Castle. "What will you do now?" demanded the emperor. "Will you conquer this city with your giant and enslave us all?"

"Would a people who celebrate the end of their own slavery wish to inflict slavery on others?" replied the rabbi. "No! Golem was created to protect the Jews. He has no other purpose."

"How long will the monster live?" asked the emperor.

"Until the Jews are no longer in danger," answered Rabbi Loew.

"Then I guarantee the safety of your people," the emperor declared. "Destroy Golem!"

"It will be done," said the rabbi. "But if we are threatened again, Golem will return, stronger than before."

The rabbi found Golem in the cemetery, gazing at the tomb-stones. "Joseph," he said softly. "Come here."

"No," said Golem.

"Why not?" asked the rabbi.

"The Jews are safe," Golem said. "Now you will return me to the earth."

"Yes," said Rabbi Loew. "Your purpose is at an end."

Golem regarded the setting sun. He raised his face to the fading light. "Father," said Golem, "will I remember this?"

"No," said Rabbi Loew. "You will be clay."

Golem leaned down to him. "Then I shall not obey you," he said.

"You have no choice, Joseph." The rabbi lashed out with his staff, erasing the first letter—*aleph*—from the word on Golem's forehead. At this, *emet*—Truth—became *met*: Death.

Golem staggered and fell to his knees. "Oh, Father!" he pleaded. "Do not do this to me!" Even as he lifted his mighty hands, they were dissolving.

"Please!" Golem cried. "Please let me live! I did all that you asked of me! Life is so . . . precious . . . to me!" With that, he collapsed into clay.

All that night, Itzak Kohen and Yakov Sassoon wheeled barrows of clay to the synagogue. They carried the clay to the attic. Rabbi Loew covered it with old *siddurs*, tattered prayer books of the congregation. Though Golem had not truly been a man, they recited Kaddish, the prayer for the dead. Then they left, locking the door behind them forever.

Since then, Golem has slept the dreamless sleep of clay. But many say he could awaken. Perhaps, when the desperate need for justice is united with holy purpose, Golem will come to life once more.

A Note

Golem (GO-lem) is the Hebrew word for "shapeless mass." In the Bible (Psalms 139:16), a form of the word describes mankind before creation: "Thine eyes did see my substance (*galmi*), yet being unperfect." In the Talmud, the revered collection of Jewish civil and sacred law, the word denotes anything imperfect or incomplete. Unconscious Adam, initially a body without a soul (*neshamah*), is referred to as a Golem. From this usage comes the Golem of medieval legend.

In Jewish tradition, to create life is to approximate the power of the Almighty. The making of a Golem could be initiated only by the most pious and righteous man, a *tzaddik* (TSAH-dik). The tzaddik must be thoroughly learned in *Cabala* (KAB-ah-lah), a mystical body of knowledge aimed at understanding the hidden nature of God and putting this understanding to practical use, to heal the sick and combat evil.

Cabalistic beliefs most likely originated with Middle Eastern sages around the year 100. They became popular in medieval times, and there are still many adherents among Hasidic Jews to this day. The basic teachings of Cabala are contained in the *Zohar*, a book written in the 1200s by the Spanish Cabalist Moses de Leon. But it is the *Sefer Yezirah* (Book of Creation), a sixth-century volume of less than two thousand words, that contains, among other formulas (*zirufim*), the one for creating a Golem. The *Sefer Yezirah* was conceived as mystical speculation (*kabbalah iyyunit*) about creation. By the eleventh century, however, it had come to be regarded as a work of practical mysticism (*kabbalah ma'asit*)—a guide to the act of creation.

According to the *Sefer Yezirah*, the giving of life was achieved by reciting combinations of the letters of the Hebrew alphabet. Because these twenty-two letters derive from the Tetragrammaton, the ineffable four-letter name of God, they possess holy power. Since God used these letters in uttering the words that created the universe, humans can wield the same forces by prayerfully mastering combinations of letters.

Judah Loew ben Bezalel (1513–1609), chief rabbi of Prague in the late sixteenth century, was a renowned Cabalist. As a *rabbi* (a blend of scholar, judge, and religious leader), he wrote extensively about religious issues, won tolerance and respect from hostile Christian clergy, and defended the Jews against unjust government decrees. Ironically, much of his fame rests upon his supposed connection with the Golem, while in fact the tales of a rabbi who created a Golem to defend his people were originally told of a Rabbi Elijah of Chelm, Poland. Only in the mid-1700s did Rabbi Loew become the subject of these stories.

This shift makes sense if one considers both Loew's reputation as a Cabalist and the occult atmosphere of Prague during Loew's time. The city was filled with alchemists and necromancers, many of them on the payroll of Emperor Rudolf II. Fascinated by the supernatural ambiance, the emperor had moved his residence from Vienna to Prague. He actually met with Rabbi Loew on February 23, 1592, possibly to discuss political matters or the virtues of astrology. Legend has made the encounter a showdown over the fate of the Golem.

The story of the Golem serves as a cautionary tale about the limits of human power. It has inspired the work of composers and authors; there is evidence of its influence in Mary Shelley's novel *Frankenstein*. The tale may even prove prophetic—as the fields of computer science, robotics, and gene manipulation advance, technological Golems may arise in our culture. But the Golem has perhaps its greatest resonance in folklore. Considering the Jewish people's long history of conflict and suffering, it is no surprise that the legend of the Golem, in which massive physical strength defeats overwhelming persecution, remains one of the most powerful traditional stories.

During centuries of conquest, strife, and exile, many Jews left Palestine. By the time of the Crusades, Jewish communities were scattered from Spain to India. This dispersion made the Jews a minority wherever they settled, and they were subjected to prejudice that took many forms. Forbidden to own land or to join craft guilds, Jews were forced into the heavily taxed and unpopular roles of minor merchants and moneylenders. They were required to wear identifying badges or other special clothing. Outrageous slanders like the Blood Lie were perpetrated against them, resulting in mob violence and appalling loss of life. Jews were not permitted to own weapons and could not defend themselves.

In many European cities, Jews were confined to walled areas called ghettos and locked in at night. Venice banished its Jews to an island where a foundry was located; the word *ghetto* is derived from the medieval Venetian word *geto*, "foundry." Not even the dead were allowed outside the ghetto walls. The tiny Jewish cemetery in Prague holds twelve thousand graves, one atop another, as many as twelve deep.

With only brief interludes of reason and tolerance, repression was all too typical of Jewish experience. Christian intolerance and political power combined to force Jewish populations from entire countries. During the thirteenth and fourteenth centuries, most Jews were driven from France and England. In 1492 all Jews were expelled from Spain. The Inquisition, a special court created by the Roman Catholic Church to punish heretics, pursued the Jews throughout the Middle Ages. In modern times, prejudice against them reached its peak in the Holocaust, the Nazi murder campaign that killed six million Jews, a third of the world's Jewish population, in the years 1939–45.

Out of this unspeakable disaster grew the impetus to establish a Jewish state. The nation of Israel was founded in 1948. Historian Jay Gonen observed in his *Psychohistory of Zionism* that, like the Golem, Israel was created to protect the physical safety of Jews through the use of physical power. In this allegorical fashion, Golem still lives.